JEFF SYPECK

Fortress of Failure: Reading F. Scott Fitzgerald's Forgotten Medievalist Stories

From 1999 to 2009, Jeff Sypeck taught medieval literature, modern science fiction and fantasy, and a course on modern medievalism for the University of Maryland University College at the College Park and Shady Grove campuses. Since 1999, he has worked as a writer and researcher for PhotoAssist, where he has helped the U.S. Postal Service develop more than 200 stamps and stamp sheets on a dizzying array of historical and cultural subjects. Born and raised in New Jersey, he now lives in an agricultural reserve in Maryland.

Fortress of Failure: Reading F. Scott Fitzgerald's Forgotten Medievalist Stories

FORTRESS OF FAILURE

Reading F. Scott Fitzgerald's Forgotten Medievalist Stories

Jeff Sypeck

QUID PLURA BOOKS
BEALLSVILLE, MARYLAND
2026

Fortress of Failure:
Reading F. Scott Fitzgerald's Forgotten Medievalist Stories

ISBN 979-8-9945226-0-8

The chapters in this book originally appeared in a slightly different form as four posts on the blog Quid Plura?, *www.quidplura.com,* from June 2018 to November 2018.

The cover design incorporates two small details from a two-page illustration by Alfred Simpkin (1898–1983) for "The Count of Darkness" in the June 1935 *Redbook* and a small section of an illustration by Jules Gotlieb (1897–?) from the opening spread of "Gods of Darkness" in the November 1941 *Redbook.* These details have been repurposed and transformed here in accordance with the principles of fair use.

No A.I. was used to research, write, or design this book.

for Michael P. Rewa,
who would have gotten
a kick out of it

CONTENTS

INTRODUCTION: *"A PIECE OF GREAT SELF INDULGENCE"*

Starting in 1934, in the waning years of his too-short life, F. Scott Fitzgerald published three medieval-themed short stories in the women's magazine *Redbook* that were followed by a fourth story in 1941, a year after his death at the age of 44. As early as 1935, Fitzgerald had envisioned a total of eight stories to round out a series he hoped to turn into a sort of comeback, a novel of ninth-century France under the working titles *The Castle* or *Philippe, Count of Darkness.*

His agent was leery. His daughter later declared the stories unworthy of being republished. Their absence from collections of Fitzgerald's work makes them sound at first like an obvious hoax. As of 2026, anyone who wants to read them has only one real option: to purchase the original issues of *Redbook,* as I did, on Ebay or from vintage magazine dealers.

The four-part essay in this little book is not a full scholarly study of Fitzgerald's medieval-themed stories. It offers an introduction to just one aspect of the unfinished Philippe saga by reading these stories through the lens of American medievalism, our ongoing tendency to rework and selectively reimagine the Middle Ages to fit our own assumptions and agendas. You won't find these pages bogged down by theory, and the style is casual, in keeping with this book's origins as four blog posts.

The work of most major American authors has been dissected into unrecognizability—but not the Philippe stories. Only a few scholars have written about or even mentioned them. The Fitzgerald estate continues to show no interest in reprinting them, and they aren't yet in the public domain in the United States. In 2021, a small publisher in the U.K. reprinted the last of the four in a limited run of 250 hand-numbered copies that sold out in less than two weeks. Genuine interest in Fitzgerald's obscure medievalist stories is a timely reminder that not everything the public wants to read is readily available online.

My intent here isn't to nitpick Fitzgerald's efforts at historical accuracy or to mock a fine writer at his lowest. The subtlety and perceptiveness of his best novels and stories become all the more apparent when his talents later forsake him, but the Philippe stories are fascinating failures for historical reasons. Although Fitzgerald struggles in the telling of these tales, they're remarkable relics of the medievalism of their times. Americans have always dreamed up their own bespoke versions of the European Middle Ages, adapting medieval stories and reinterpreting myth, history, and legend to suit the mood of the moment. Finding out that Fitzgerald likewise trod this weird path, even as it led him astray, illuminates from a strange new angle an author we thought we knew.

Fitzgerald sensed that deep mysteries in the faux-medieval architecture of his college campus connected the present with the past, and his fascination with the Middle Ages lasted the rest of his life. My hope is that this little book nudges others to revive the conversation about Fitzgerald as a literary medievalist. Readers may not find themselves moved by the stories he himself dubbed "a piece of great self indulgence," but even the plainest heap of medieval potsherds has stories it's waiting to tell.

Beallsville, Maryland
February 2026

1: INSUFFICIENT SCHEMES

"In the Darkest Hour," *Redbook,* October 1934

The footnote jumped out at me like a desperate spark from an otherwise dwindling fire. The scholar had dismissed what I considered a marvel, rushing past it with such haste that he obviously never dreamed that anyone might want to know more. I'd long been interested in rooting out medievalism in unexpected corners of American life, but it hadn't occurred to me that F. Scott Fitzgerald, of all authors, might be obsessed with writing stories set in Carolingian Europe.

The Philippe stories take effort to locate and patience to read. Fitzgerald's daughter thought they were awful and deemed them unreprintable.[1] I tracked down the back issues of *Redbook* on Ebay, half-expecting to discover the El Dorado of American medievalism, delusional legends that inspired only folly—and in a week a magazine was in my hands, the

October 1934 *Redbook* with the first Philippe story, "In the Darkest Hour," paired with evocative illustrations by Saul Tepper that make you long for much greater artistry from the facing-page ads for soup, sink cleaner, and booze.

"In the Darkest Hour" is so unlike anything I'd read by Fitzgerald that if I hadn't seen his name on the crumbling magazine cover, I never would have believed he'd written it.

The plot is simple. It's A.D. 872 in the Loire valley, and Philippe, who was whisked away to Andalusia as a child and raised as the stepson of the Muslim vizier, returns to Villefranche as an adult to reclaim his ancestral lands and fulfill his duties as the rightful count. When he finds his homeland ravaged by Vikings and his ignorant subjects scrounging through rubble, he rallies a small band of dubious locals, instructs them in rudimentary horsemanship, and sets them up on mules and donkeys to become, in Fitzgerald's words,

> *as grotesque a caricature of chivalry as can be imagined. Nevertheless, mounted were they all, after a fashion; and Philippe's idea was a prefiguration of an age already beginning, when mounted men were to take over the shaping of feudal Europe.*

Philippe's pathetic remnant defeats a small band of predatory Norsemen, inspired in part by their count's promise: He'll protect his people and keep the peace in exchange for their good service. Thus by one man, sayeth Fitzgerald, is feudalism born:

> *There are epochs when certain things sing in the air, and certain strong courageous men hear them intuitively long before the rest. This was an epoch of disturbance and change; all over Europe men were thinking exactly like Philippe, taking directions from the arrows of history that seemed to float dimly overhead. Each of those men thought himself to be alone, but really each was an instrument of response to a great human need. Each knew that the spirit of man was at low tide; each one felt in himself the necessity of seizing power by force and cunning.*

This might be wieldy stuff in the hands of a practiced pulp writer like "Conan" creator Robert E. Howard, who knew how to feed his readers' appetites for vivid, thrilling tales. They expected to smell a dank battlefield, feel the rough grip of a spear, and wade through the muck in realms ruled by muscle and brawn. The best pulp writers were enwound in their worldviews and knew without doubt what they wanted to say. Fitzgerald isn't at home here. In "certain things sing in the air," "certain things" should be more specific, more evocative of the medieval mind, ideally through imagery that suggests actual song. Arrows, though deadly, are too small and fragile to represent the larger forces of history when used so concretely. Saying they only "seemed to float" overhead (rather than speed, whistle, rush, or fly) makes for a weak, feeble image. "An instrument of response" evokes nothing specific; a civilizational "low tide" is a cliché.

And then, after a climactic battle that ought to leave us feeling as if civilization itself is at stake, Fitzgerald observes lazily: "It was a busy day."

Readers of "In the Darkest Hour" will search in vain for one sentence that's even somewhat worthy of the author of *The Great Gatsby*. You *will* find unexpected hoards of dialect, as characters speak like hardboiled 1930s gangsters transported to a poker table in the Old West. Philippe greets the first person he sees with "Howdy! God save you!" and asks "hey, where's this place at?" When a monk is reluctant to join the fight, Philippe thinks "he's yellow!" and tells the monk he plans "to protect the jakes." One local declares: "High time somebody did somethin' around here. Everything's rottin' away."

I suppose Fitzgerald wants the anachronistic dialect to draw meaningful connections between 1934 and 872, but it's neither consistent nor emphatic enough to conjure the wisp of a metaphor. In addition to Philippe the Franco-Andalusian expat, we also meet Irish monks, French peasants, and Norsemen, all of whom distrust each other based on differences in appearance and speech. Fitzgerald is admirably aware, perhaps too aware, that early medieval Europe wasn't culturally homogeneous, but in a story that otherwise says everything and implies nothing—"[i]t was a desolate countryside, the more so, as there was evidence here and there that it had been once been highly cultivated"—he doesn't give us a hint as to what he thinks this clash of cultures ought to mean in 1934.

Fitzgerald's fascination with the Middle Ages surprised me, but maybe it shouldn't have. Raised in a Catholic family, he spent his truncated college career at Princeton, where he read Oswald Spengler's *Decline of the West* and volumes of early Celtic history on a campus that had lately sprouted acres of neo-Gothic halls. By the time he published "In the Darkest Hour" in 1934, American museums were busily expanding their medieval collections, cranky medievalist church and college architect Ralph Adams Cram had been featured on the cover of *Time* magazine, and the *New York Times* was reporting that 370,000 children nationwide were enrolled in youth clubs that preached the virtues of knighthood and chivalry.[2]

We think of Fitzgerald as a chronicler of his times, but he hoped, I think, to understand the follies of his era in a much grander scheme, and not only in the Philippe stories. In *The Medievalist Impulse in American Literature: Twain, Adams, Fitzgerald, and Hemingway*, Kim Moreland argues that Jay Gatsby is a modern adherent of medieval courtly love. Gatsby navigates a set of rules in the service of adultery and practices a religion of love, "a commitment to the dream, the ideal, the essential, rather than the material, the accidental, the existential...a desire for mystical transcendence."

According to Moreland, Fitzgerald's own fleur-de-lys fancies eventually withered:

> *In his novels Fitzgerald explores the cost of a modern allegiance to the courtly model. Yet the validity of the model itself is not seriously called into question. Only in Fitzgerald's unfinished last novel,* The Last Tycoon, *does he suggest that the male protagonist perhaps errs in desiring a courtly relationship, that his desire for a courtly lady rather than a modern woman might be misbegotten.*[3]

In need of new *matière,* Fitzgerald looked again to the Middle Ages and wrote—what? "In the Darkest Hour" isn't sufficiently lurid to join the ranks of even the middling historical pulp fiction of its era. You'd never suspect that the author of this flat, prolix story had written sentence after eloquent sentence in *Gatsby,* a novel that reveres the reader's powers of inference. Did something other than escapism make a keen observer of his own times look back a thousand years for fresh new things to say?

An editorial note at the end of the story offers a clue: "F. Scott Fitzgerald has written another vivid drama of the dark ages *[sic]* which even more significantly illuminates recent events in Europe and which will appear in an early issue." Almost nobody delves into medievalism because they wish they had lived in the real Middle Ages. Like many before him and many since, Fitzgerald grabs at a medieval metaphor to help him make sense of the here and now. But is the devastated and chaotic Loire valley of "In the Darkest Hour" the Europe of rising fascism and Nazism? A nation wrecked by the Great Depression? An America altered by immigration? Little in the story itself encourages even a charitable reader to see anything but stilted actors in medieval dress.

But then there's this, a remarkable jotting from Fitzgerald's own notes: "Just as Stendahl's portrait of a Byronic man made *Le Rouge et Noir* so couldn't *my* portrait of Ernest as Philippe make the real modern man."[4] Yes, "Ernest," *that* Ernest: Fitzgerald's Philippe, the Andalusian-bred French nobleman, is Ernest Hemingway transported to early medieval Europe, where he'll crack some skulls and rebuild civilization, with his own bare hands if necessary.

Cheerless after his first modest victory, Philippe holds vigil while weaker men sleep: "Let the others get tired," he sneers. "I keep the watch." The evocative closing line of "In the Darkest Hour" sets up Philippe as an indispensable savior: "Embodying in himself alone the future of his race, he walked to and fro in the starry darkness."

The future of his race. The human race? Christian Europe? Or just the medieval French? As a stand-in for what or for whom? Does it matter that Philippe has blue-blooded authority but is a stranger in his own land? What so ails the world in 1934 that Ernest Hemingway in medieval kit is the only man who can save it?

Such questions may be futile. One scholar has called the publication of the Philippe stories by *Redbook* "an act of charity toward an author in decline."[5] I don't doubt he's right, but reading these stories may be worth the slog—not to sully the memory of Fitzgerald, whose best work sets him safely beyond embarrassment, but to figure out what inspired his obsessive rooting through the rubble of medieval Europe. What was he was looking for, and why did he fail so badly to find it?

2: WHISPER TALES OF GORE

"The Count of Darkness," ***Redbook,*** **June 1935**

Fitzgerald's second Philippe story in the June 1935 *Redbook* begins with an editor's lie: "The brilliant thought quality and style of the creator of 'The Great Gatsby' are very much in evidence in this majestic story of 879 A.D." Two lies, really: By design, there's nothing "majestic" about "The Count of Darkness." Fitzgerald wallows in sketching out civilization at its lowest ebb, but his version of the Middle Ages yields more than he's able to confront.

When last we checked in with Philippe in October 1934, Fitzgerald had dropped Ernest Hemingway into ninth-century France, dressing him up as a noble exile-hostage returning from Spain to France to reclaim both land and leadership. While the story picks up only a day or so after Philippe has rallied a scruffy band of locals, routed a band of Northmen, and invented feudalism in his spare time, *Redbook* editors have made generous presumptions about their readers' lingering interest after an eight-month gap.

Fitzgerald opens "The Count of Darkness" with one of the better stabs at adequate writing in the series so far:

> *It was a cold dawn. Over the low hills it was iridescent, opalescent, then flowing into morning. The master of the domain, who had eventually fallen off to sleep against a wagon-wheel, woke quickly—under the impression that he was attacked. The prospect of the Tourainian countryside was so lovely that he could not again compose himself to rest—this fact, adjoined to the fact of his so recent conquest of the farmers' allegiance. Not yet could he count on their adherence to him in principle. And he was no one for taking chances.*

That paragraph is far from elegant. Fitzgerald tells more than he shows: "iridescent" and "opalescent" give us only adjectives, not images; "under the impression that he was attacked" conveys no real sense of alarm; and the pedantic clarity of "this fact, adjoined to the fact" is at odds with Philippe's groggy restlessness. Still, I can hear faint traces of Fitzgerald in those sentences, calling upon the ghost of his former gifts in a desperate effort to set a suitable mood.

But then Philippe strikes up a conversation with a 17-year-old Aquitanian girl, and things get weird:

> *"What do you want, little chicken?" he asked.*
>
> *"I wanted to see you. I could only see you a little from the tent, and—"*
>
> *"Don't grovel in the dirt, for God's sake! Get up from your knees!"*
>
> *"I'm not a man." She stood and faced him. "How do I know about your habits for gals?"*
>
> *"There* are *no habits—I* make *the habits."*
>
> *His eyes had become covetous as he looked at her. "How would you like to become one of my habits?"*
>
> *"Oh, sire, I would be so glad to be yours—"*
>
> *"What's your name, little baggage?"*
>
> *"Letgarde."*
>
> *"Who gave it to you? That Norman?"*
>
> *"It was my christened name."*
>
> *"Come here and see what you taste like."*
>
> *After a while he released her with:*
>
> *"I've met worse kids. How you going* [sic] *earn your keep? Can you get together some stew from the rations in the wagon—if we get up a couple boys to do the heavy stuff?"*
>
> *"I'll try it, darl—"*
>
> *"Call me 'Sire'! . . . And remember: There's no bedroom talk floating around this precinct!"*

> *"All right, darl—I mean sire."*
> *"Well, run along."*

Maybe we're supposed to hear the voices of a 1930s gangster and his moll, perhaps a dash of Damon Runyon—but are "chicken" and "baggage" 1930s slang, or are they Fitzgerald's way of sounding "medieval"? In the first story, Philippe was stern and humorless. Is he still a grim, flinty strongman, or is he flirting here? In *The Great Gatsby,* telling moments arise when the narrator elides a potentially revealing or uncomfortable event, so again I see the old Fitzgerald in the "[a]fter a while he released her" line, which invites us to fill in the blanks, but it's clunky and obvious, and it fosters no sympathy for Philippe.

Maybe that's the point. Philippe's second act that morning is to find women who can cook and clean for the men in his nascent army. He later addresses what he considers a "minor problem":

> *announcing to the half-dozen girls who had been rounded up that for the moment each would be permitted her parents' hut for the night, but that in the future there would be no marriage permitted in the country save with his permission. He would expect them to choose their mates among his own men.*

Later, when Philippe spots a Syrian caravan fording his river, he first proposes robbing the merchants before downgrading his plan to extorting the heck out of them. Fitzgerald has a lurid preoccupation with how nasty and brutish people become when civilization shatters. He wants to shock and enlighten the magazine-reading public of 1935, like the Ivy League freshman home for Thanksgiving who demonstrates whole weeks of superior wisdom to largely indifferent relatives.

Even so, "The Count of Darkness" isn't a retread of the previous story, but a dramatization of the setbacks in Philippe's campaign to renew the world. Philippe focuses so coldly on surveying land for a hill fort that he neglects the niceties that hold civilization together:

> *Catching the beast and saddling him, he pulled Letgarde up with him after he had mounted. The force of his pull almost wrenched her arm from its socket.*
>
> *Smarting with sudden rage at the indignity, she waited in fright as, guiding the animal with his legs only, he next swung her about from a position facing him, to one that would later be called postilion. Furious and uncomfortable, she rode off behind him toward a destination of which she knew nothing. Perforce she clung to his body.*
>
> *"Don't let go, baby, and nothing can happen to you."*

Tasked with watching from a hilltop and signaling if she sees marauders, Letgarde bails:

> *He had scarcely gone galloping toward the other hill when Letgarde, quivering with indignation, set off on a dead run back to the wagons. She had never, from the most ruthless marauder, received such treatment—and she did not understand it. She came from a civilized province of old Roman Gaul. The Norse chief who had adopted her was little more than a sugar-daddy—he treated her always as a sort of queen.*
>
> *But this man!*

When Letgarde vanishes, rumored to have run off with a wandering singer, her memory haunts Philippe. He thinks he glimpses her through the trees, ghostly and hateful, and he can't shake off a peasant's story about "some nutsy girl down-stream that lives on a little island and thinks she's Venus or something." But in the midst of his obsessive fishing—a nighttime spear-hunt for eels that made me jot "Hemingway leaves Spain to fish in medieval France" in my notes—he and his men behold a baleful sight:

> *Philippe's voice was almost blasphemous on the dark tide, the lovely surface mirroring a round full moon, till—*

> *"Oh my God in heaven!" he cried.*
>
> *And then:*
>
> *"Don't you see?"*
>
> *On the breast of the water rode the body of a girl; she was attired in only a shift, and for a moment she gave an appearance almost lifelike. Philippe pulled her into the glossy surface, illumined her by candles on the dark bank.*

Philippe's reaction is one of the few genuine surprises in this story. When a henchman reveals that Letgarde had been waiting desperately in this spot for the rain-swollen river to subside so she could cross, Philippe snaps:

> *Straight as straight, Philippe threw his ax at the man's head. It hit, cleaved, biting deep, and Philippe went over with his sword and dispatched him. Then he turned to the others:*
>
> *"Nobody told me this!"*

Fitzgerald is on the verge of layering his medievalism to interesting effect: He takes the basic Astolat/Shalott motif, drenched as it is in medieval notions of love perfumed with Victorian romanticism, and makes it unexpectedly useful in what could have been a passable pulp yarn for early 20th-century men—and then he wrecks it. Letgarde's avoidable death, Philippe's fondness for her, his apparent liberty to murder his subjects in anger—Fitzgerald doesn't let any of it resonate:

> *"When I got tough on you, you decided to go off with that gang—and you tried to find another ford? And you got stuck? And you got killed—so you wouldn't have to come back to me!"*
>
> *He picked up her body and rocked it to and fro.*
>
> *"Poor little lost doggy—if you could have taken it a little better, you'd maybe be queen of these parts."*
>
> *Inert, her body slid from him; almost as inert, he retreated to a birch tree.*
>
> *"She followed that damn' tramp," he thought, "just because I used her rough on the horse when I was in a hurry."*

By explaining every emotion, Fitzgerald leaves readers nothing to infer, no connections to make, no implications to ponder. When Philippe, "choked with emotion" and "lost in sorrowful contemplation," meets an orphan outside his fort and adopts her as his own daughter, he tells his majordomo that the girl will be "sacred here forever." Thus do we cross the river into a new realm of hokey sentimentality.

"The Count of Darkness" badly makes worthy points: Leadership is a burden, but its responsibilities include pragmatism and mercy, and warriors alone can't bring civilization to fruition. Even amid chaos be mindful, Fitzgerald says, of the possibilities of love and affection, not just utilitarian arrangements, and remember that expedience is not necessarily wisdom. To that end, the story includes appearances by a wandering minstrel whom Philippe contemptuously calls a "hobo" and a "singing tramp." At first I thought the singer was Fitzgerald's way of suggesting how frivolous the arts must seem when people are starving, but maybe he felt similarly marginal as a writer by 1935, warbling in a world with no use for his particular tunes.

As the second Philippe story ends, Fitzgerald's medieval stories have told us less about his perspective on the 1930s and more about his own fears. I assumed he would use the Middle Ages only as a metaphor for the fragility of civilization, allowing him to trot out an example of the sort of rough man he believed could save or rebuild it, but his veer into sentimentality makes me think he found more in the past than his plan for the Philippe tales could accommodate. Most writers and artists who dabble in medievalism find their own highly selective version of the Middle Ages, usually the version they went looking for in the first place, but Fitzgerald wades into the ninth century and can't make sense of it. That doesn't necessarily make "The Count of Darkness" an interesting failure, but it does make it an honest one, underneath the kitsch.

3: AND THEY BURN SO BRIGHT

"The Kingdom in the Dark," ***Redbook,*** **August 1935**

F. Scott Fitzgerald's third story about medieval France "shows that national chaos does not fail to bring forth a leader." That's the chirpy editorial comment just below the byline in the August 1935 issue of *Redbook,* and it makes me wonder if the magazine's staffers actually read the story. By now, they're no longer touting Fitzgerald's contributions on the covers, so readers would have had to stumble upon "The Kingdom in the Dark" while flipping through an issue already packed with other, lighter fiction. I wonder how many of them even remembered where the story of Count Philippe of Villefranche left off eleven months earlier.

Yet Fitzgerald's name still carries cachet for *Redbook* readers. Elsewhere in the issue, his name pops up in the introduction to a novel presented in full, *We'll Never Be Any Younger:*

> *WHAT F. SCOTT FITZGERALD DID FOR THE "LOST GENERATION"—FOR "FLAPPERS" AND "SAD YOUNG MEN"—IN "THIS SIDE OF PARADISE" AND "THE GREAT GATSBY," ELMER DAVIS IS DOING NOW FOR THOSE WHO ARE LIVING UNDER THE SIGN OF ALPHABET AGENCIES AND GREAT PROMISES.*

That's a kind endorsement of Fitzgerald's influence, but it's also a backhanded compliment that casts Fitzgerald as a has-been, a generational spokesman receding into mere precedent. It makes sense then that his medieval stories would dramatize rebuilding a world from scratch and the unavoidable failures that follow.

As with Fitzgerald's previous medieval stories, "The Kingdom in the Dark" isn't encumbered by a complicated plot. Count Philippe continues to consolidate power on his hereditary lands by building a fort overlooking the Loire, where he can collect tolls and taxes from merchants who ford the river. There's a charming, boyish innocence to Fitzgerald's pride in writing about this fort, which is clearly the product of his own historical research:

> *Philippe had no education in military architecture, and probably any engineer-centurion of Caesar's army would have laughed it to scorn, yet he had planned with a great deal of shrewdness:*
>
> *To the north the hill fell straight to the river; westward it was protected by a sheer cliff fifty feet high. The vulnerable points were east and south. It was with the eastward side, a slope of shifting sandy soil that would bear no solid construction, that he was unsatisfied...*

Later, Philippe explains the fort to the local abbot:

> *"Father couldn't defend his house, God rest his soul! But I have an idea that the Northmen will have some job trying to crack this crib in a hurry. Look—this thing is only the first palisade—then there's a second palisade, then the rampart and trench. On two of the other sides I've got the river and the cliff."*

Then Fitzgerald gives us an arid historical lecture on ninth-century forts:

> *In an hour they were in sight of the house or fort. Land was easy to get in those unsettled days, but the ability to dominate and cultivate it was another matter. The prohibition of forts and*

castles had only just been withdrawn by the king, in the face of repeated invasions of Northmen; and though this law had not been observed literally for a half century, the art of fortification had fallen into desuetude.

Finally, Philippe shows off his fort to a girl:

> *"Like it?" Philippe asked the girl, with ill-concealed pride.*
>
> *"I think it's fine," she said, and took a side glance at him, with pity for his pride in his homely effort.*
>
> *"It's not so good," he said, with the modesty of possession. "Still, we've got three buildings up there—there's the log fort and the houses for my men-at-arms and servants made of mud and rock. They're part of the defenses."*
>
> *"It's nice."*
>
> *She looked at him as a little boy playing soldiers, and for a moment they regarded each other. Then, reluctantly, he turned his eyes from the lovely head.*

Fortunately, "The Kingdom in the Dark" isn't entirely about forts. Philippe is intrigued by the girl, Griselda, who's on the run from the new king, Louis the Stammerer, apparently because he made her lover in his court disappear. Fitzgerald's description of her isn't terrible, but it's the kind of prose that earns aspiring fantasy novelists a gentle critique from their peers:

> *The girl rode well. Her rather small curly head perched on a long body that carried it proudly. She was pale, and her lips were very red. There was a lovely necklace of faint freckles above an amber-colored surtout belted at the waist. Her eyes were small and hazel, with lashes of a delicate pink tan.*

Nothing in this description of Griselda tells us anything useful about her. Can this really be the same novelist who could imply so much about Gatsby and his acquaintances through subtle descriptions of posture and clothing?

Fitzgerald revels in costuming, but little else, in an interminable passage about the king's entourage:

> *To a man of our time, associating the Middle Ages with plate mail, the column would have seemed singularly dissimilar to any mental picture he might have formed of chivalry—and it was not chivalry in the sense that the word implied five hundred years later.*
>
> *At the head of the procession rode a squad of scouts, carrying short spears, and short flat swords slung at their belts. Some wore cap-like padded helmets, turbans almost; others wore*

headgear of the same shape but of leather. There was no attempt at uniformity—under short tunics of blue, red, green or brown, there was usually perceptible a rough mail: rings sewed on leather, or crude coats of rings entire. Universally they wore leather moccasins, short or long, held in place by crisscross strips of hide.

After this casual advance party followed the King and his attendants—Louis in a long white tunic of fine linen shouldered with a cape of purple. Round his head was a light golden circlet; around his middle a golden chain of flexible links from which swung a flat jeweled sword . . .

King Louis was flanked by a gray-haired knight and an ecclesiastic. Following them came a quartet of esquires, then about sixty horsemen, dressed with as little uniformity as the advance guard . . . Then came the supply wagons, drawn by huge horses instead of oxen, and driven by men who served also as cooks and sutlers. A group of horsemen, well armed and knightly of bearing, brought up the rear.

Are you still awake? Anyone who's written historical fiction or popular nonfiction knows what's going on here: Fitzgerald has done his homework, and by God, he's going to exhaust every last scrap of his notes. It's painful to behold, all the more because he opens this pageant with a paragraph that only distances the reader from the medieval world. We're glancing backward through time at a museum diorama of costumed mannequins, not characters we want to care about.

Briefly, Fitzgerald catches sight of an intriguing moral conflict: Philippe conceals Griselda from a cruel, absurd king, even though he ought to be loyal to him, and even though Griselda has stolen one of the king's horses. Philippe swears falsely that he knows nothing about her—when he does, Fitzgerald tells us that "invisible girths tightened on Philippe's diaphragm"—but this false oath would have potentially interesting implications only in a more thoughtful story.

Instead, the king's men burn down Philippe's precious fort, Philippe executes the conspirators, and the gloomy count spends just two sentences wondering if he's being punished:

> *"I took a false oath this morning, and maybe Almighty Providence doesn't believe me anymore. But someday, by God, I'll build a fort of stone that all the kings of Christendom can't burn up or knock down!"*

Is this a moment of heroic defiance, or hypocritical futility? Beats me. There's no sense of Providence in this story, no appeal to truth, no sense that anything matters in "The Kingdom in the Dark" but brute force.

"But Philippe was wasting his passion," Fitzgerald writes. "Three days later Louis the Stammerer, King of the West Franks, obligingly died." That's the final line of the story, a conclusion that snuffs out whatever embers of tension and conflict Fitzgerald has spent nine pages trying to kindle.

"The Kingdom in the Dark" is an unsatisfying mess, but I'd be a lazy reader if I didn't dig for more. The jarring, meaningless ending doesn't have to be a sign that Fitzgerald, like Philippe, was "wasting his passion." Maybe the closing of the story is a statement in itself, Fitzgerald's implication that history doesn't unfold in a coherent narrative.

For some writers, the Middle Ages are an admirably pure foil to the miserable complexity of the modern world—or they're a era of ignorance that reflects our own superior wisdom, or a supposed source of cultural origins, or a period that highlights timeless aspects of human nature, or a setting whose violence bestows "authenticity," or a distant carnival of irreproducible human strangeness. Novels, movies, and TV shows cover all this ground, but Fitzgerald's may be one of the bleakest fictionalizations of the Middle Ages I've come across. In his vision of ninth-century France, he can't imagine spontaneous human organization or the persistence of culture. After Viking raiders blast the landscape to rubble, the locals are reduced to helpless savages. Only a strong nobleman can motivate them and impose order.

Yet even Philippe falters: When the destruction of his fort tempts him to despair, he considers joining the Norsemen as a mercenary. Only his new squeeze, Griselda, brings out the best in him, insisting that he has a responsibility to his subjects and reminding him that one can hate the king as a person but still be loyal to him. It's the second time a woman has tempered Philippe with reason and softened his heart. In "The Kingdom in the Dark," he gets noticeably nicer, showing a genial rapport with his majordomo and the local abbot that was absent from earlier stories.

Even so, this is a tale in which the hero who rebuilds civilization will defy his king, swear false oaths, and ignore laws that aren't of his own devising. In his notes, Fitzgerald wrote that the character of Philippe, inspired by Ernest Hemingway, was meant to represent the "modern man,"[6] but three stories in, the likeness isn't flattering. Modern stories set in the Middle Ages inevitably comment on the present. Is Fitzgerald rationalizing corruption if it's for a good cause in desperate times? Is his medieval world a warning, or a template he thinks we'll someday require? I can't tell; I don't think Fitzgerald knew either.

4: THE WITCH'S PROMISE

"Gods of Darkness," *Redbook*, November 1941

Six years passed between the publication of the third Philippe story and the fourth and final entry in the series. By the time "Gods of Darkness" debuted in the November 1941 issue of *Redbook*—which hailed the seven-page sketch as its "novelette of the month"—Fitzgerald had been dead for almost a year. According to scholar Janet Lewis, *Redbook* had been the only magazine willing to print the stories, and I'm guessing they ran the final installment out of some combination of nostalgic tribute and contractual obligation.

A reader who's made it this far into the Philippe stories knows what's coming. There's the ninth-century warlord inspired by Ernest Hemingway, the anachronistic 1930s slang, the prose that hastily tells and never shows, and a boyish—and by now cloying—obsession with the building and maintenance of forts.

I'm not kidding about the forts:

> *Half a dozen horsemen, irregularly strung out, began feeling their way down the forty-five-degree angle of the slag-and-sand slope.*
>
> *"That's my fort," Philippe said. "You like it?"*
>
> *[. . .]*
>
> *In sight of the castle he had made on the hilltop, he drew rein for a moment, to reward his own work admiringly. New wooden structure was risen to replace the first crude one, destroyed by the King's incendiaries. This one, like the first, was of logs, but it was taller, more elaborate within and without. His current problem was to try to make a moat by letting in the Loire; but having no engineering education, and commanding no one who understood the process, the venture had so far been confined to digging fine-looking ditches and then seeing them either washed quickly away, or else coquettishly avoided by the choosy water of the river.*
>
> *"It's good, though, isn't it?" he demanded of Griselda. "We've got a house; we've got quarters for the boys; we've got pasture for the animals—and we're beginning to have a little city down*

here around the foot of the hill. There's ten, twelve houses...."

If Fitzgerald had spent even half as many words exploring the conflicting subtleties of his version of the medieval mind, the Philippe stories might feel inhabited by humans. Instead, the banter between Philippe and Griselda is as flat as a scene from a 1930s "B" movie:

> *Griselda, fatigued, dismounted in the pasture halfway up. Pale and lovely, she sat in the last lush grass of October.*
>
> *"I love you, Philippe," she said as he dismounted beside her. "Oh, I don't mean that—I was just thinking: can't I love you sometimes when you don't expect it?"*
>
> *The pale wonder of her skin was a texture so like death that for a moment Philippe hardly knew what he held in his suddenly gentle arms. Only when a bearer of water had come and returned, did Griselda move and whisper: "I know I'm difficult, Philippe; but you're so difficult, and I never had anything like this happen to me before."*
>
> *"Cheer up—you're all right," said Philippe. He had a dread of anything happening to her delicate health.*

Despite his oppressive deadpan, Fitzgerald tries to be playful, to no real end. "In less time than it has taken to describe Philippe's bodyguard, he met the approaching party," he writes, a wink from a narrator rarely inclined to step forward with self-referential quips. I can't be the first reader to wish that the Philippe stories were filtered through the eyes of an observer, a ninth-century Nick Carraway who could have given Fitzgerald's version of the Middle Ages a solid sense of place.

Fortunately, "Gods of Darkness" delivers a plot twist that at least earns points for novelty. In the months Fitzgerald spent immersed in scholarly books and working out his historical timelines, he was beguiled by Margaret Murray's 1921 book *The Witch-Cult in Western Europe.* As Philippe becomes a competent ruler of his ancestral lands, he realizes that his girlfriend and his henchman both speak a strange language and hold secret influence over the locals. His military prowess and burgeoning administrative skills will mean nothing unless he allies himself with an unpredictable faction, the local witch cult:

> *"I haven't got any conscience except for my country, and for those who live in it. All right—I'll use this cult—and maybe burn in hell forever after...But maybe Almighty Providence will understand." He looked toward the swift flow of the Loire. "Maybe*

He built a castle once. Maybe He knows."

And then defiantly:

"But if these witches know better, then I'll be one of them!"

If Fitzgerald had stopped at "Maybe He knows," Philippe might have become a broken-down idealist worthy of noir. Instead, the big, dumb warlord bellows his intentions, ruining a moment when Fitzgerald might have respected his readers' capacity for inference. We're detached from the fate of a character we've barely been persuaded to care about, with none of the thrilling gut-punch of genuine pulp.

In one of the few scholarly studies of the "Count of Darkness" series, Janet Lewis floats a theory: Philippe's compromises are an allegory for the need of the United States to team up with the Soviet Union to defeat Hitler. The *Redbook* issue with "Gods of Darkness" hit the stands a few weeks before Pearl Harbor, so some readers may have seen it that way, and the notion wouldn't have been unfamiliar to them, but these stories feel less like political exhortations than clumsy studies of people dealing with dark times.

Perhaps any sociopolitical echo is accidental: Fitzgerald told editor Maxwell Perkins that he enjoyed the escapism of writing about medieval Europe, even if it was risky to write a massive novel that revisited Philippe at three phases of his 60-year career. "The research required for the second two parts would be quite tremendous," Fitzgerald confessed, "and the book would have been (or would be) a piece of great self indulgence."[7]

The Philippe stories *are* self-indulgent, and their rare readers end up disappointed or indifferent. Yet I haven't seen anyone appreciate that Fitzgerald may be careening toward an obvious conclusion: that if you drop Ernest Hemingway into the crucible of boundless chaos and war, he may seem at first like the sort of man to rebuild the world. Then he'll get in over his head, and he'll end up believing in nothing.

* * *

The Philippe stories might be more revealing if we read them alongside Fitzgerald's other work. After the letdown of "Gods of Darkness," I went back to *This Side of Paradise,* his 1920 debut novel. For the medievalist, the highlight of Chapter Two, "Spires and Gargoyles," is a passage with its own precocious subtitle, "A Damp Symbolic Interlude," the musings of Princeton underachiever Amory Blaine as he wanders the campus:

> *The night mist fell. From the moon it rolled, clustered about the spires and towers, and then settled below them, so that the dreaming peaks were still in lofty aspiration toward the sky. Figures that dotted the day like ants now brushed along as shadowy ghosts, in and out*

of the foreground. The Gothic halls and cloisters were infinitely more mysterious as they loomed suddenly out of the darkness, outlined each by myriad faint squares of yellow light. Indefinitely from somewhere a bell boomed the quarter-hour, and Amory, pausing by the sun-dial, stretched himself out full length on the damp grass. The cool bathed his eyes and slowed the flight of time—time that had crept so insidiously through the lazy April afternoons, seemed so intangible in the long spring twilights. Evening after evening the senior singing had drifted over the campus in melancholy beauty, and through the shell of his undergraduate consciousness had broken a deep and reverent devotion to the gray walls and Gothic peaks and all they symbolized as warehouses of dead ages.

The tower that in view of his window sprang upward, grew into a spire, yearning higher until its uppermost tip was half invisible against the morning skies, gave him the first sense of the transiency and unimportance of the campus figures except as holders of the apostolic succession. He liked knowing that Gothic architecture, with its upward trend, was peculiarly appropriate to universities, and the idea became personal to him. The silent stretches of green, the quiet halls with an occasional late-

burning scholastic light held his imagination in a strong grasp, and the chastity of the spire became a symbol of this perception.

"Damn it all," he whispered aloud, wetting his hands in the damp and running them through his hair. "Next year I work!" Yet he knew that where now the spirit of spires and towers made him dreamily acquiescent, it would then overawe him. Where now he realized only his own inconsequence, effort would make him aware of his own impotency and insufficiency.

The college dreamed on—awake.

Look at what Fitzgerald can do when he knows what he's doing. To a status-addled Princeton undergrad, the Gothic embodies imagination, ambition, humility, and the weight of tradition all at once. A rainy walk across campus makes the heart swell with giddy confusion. Those three paragraphs show a sensitivity to human emotion wholly absent from dozens of pages about warlords and fort-building.

The nod to Gothic architecture is also a sign of the times. When Fitzgerald attended Princeton from 1913 to 1917, the campus's oldest Gothic spires were still fairly new, having been built only after the Civil War, and many of the gargoyles had been leering down at cocky undergrads for only three or four years. Fitzgerald knows to tap into not only the romanticism of Gothic

Revival architecture but also its pretensions. He later failed to make sense of the 1930s through the lens of medievalism, but he long understood that the Middle Ages were potentially fertile ground for ambiguous symbolism and complex allusions.

You wouldn't know it if you've read only *The Great Gatsby*, but Fitzgerald was long haunted by medieval shadows. His biggest failure in the "Philippe, Count of Darkness" stories is his inability to decide whether the Middle Ages were a warning about the problems of his own age or the beginning of a way out of them. The mind of a Jazz Age author turns out to have been a Gothic novel: enter the mansion, get lost deep beneath it in medieval crypts.

NOTES

1: West, xviii
2: Lupack, 59–60
3: Moreland, 157
4: Tate, 47–48
5: Crawford, 12
6: Tate, 48
7: Turnbull, 283

BIBLIOGRAPHY

Curious readers can track down the Philippe stories in these issues of *Redbook:*

"In the Darkest Hour." *Redbook,* October 1934: 15–19, 94–98.

"The Count of Darkness." *Redbook,* June 1935: 20–23, 68, 70, 72.

"The Kingdom in the Dark." *Redbook,* August 1935: 58–62, 64, 66–68.

"Gods of Darkness." *Redbook,* November 1941: 30–33, 88–91.

"Gods of Darkness" was reprinted in 2021 in a limited edition of 250 by Sangrail Press (see Newell, below).

This bibliography includes the works cited in this book as well as other examples of scholarship on the Philippe stories to give new researchers a few starting points.

Bruccoli, Matthew J. *Some Sort of Epic Grandeur: The Life of F. Scott Fitzgerald.* Boston: Da Capo Press, 1993.

Crawford, Dan. "'Count of Darkness'—A great writer's least-read work." *Caxtonian: Journal of the Caxton Club of Chicago* 11:9 (September 2003): 12–13.

Lewis, Janet. "Fitzgerald's 'Philippe, Count of Darkness.'" *Fitzgerald/Hemingway Annual 1975:* 7–32.

Lupack, Alan. "Visions of Courageous Achievement: Arthurian Youth Groups in America." *Studies in Medievalism VI: Medievalism in North America* (1994): 50–68.

Moreland, Kim. *The Medievalist Impulse in American Literature: Twain, Adams, Fitzgerald, and Hemingway.* Charlottesville: University Press of Virginia, 1996.

Moyer, Kermit W. "Fitzgerald's Two Unfinished Novels: The Count and the Tycoon in Spenglerian

Perspective." *Contemporary Literature* 15:2 (spring 1974): 238–256.

Newell, Adam. "Fitzgerald, Lovecraft, and the Witch Cult Connection." In F. Scott Fitzgerald, *Gods of Darkness*. Penrith, Cumbria: Sangrail Press, 2021: 23–35.

Stoneback, H.R. "A Dark Ill-Lighted Place: Fitzgerald and Hemingway, Philippe Count of Darkness and Philip Counter-Espionage Agent." In Bryer, Jackson R., Alan Margolies, and Ruth Prigozy, eds. *F. Scott Fitzgerald: New Perspectives*. Athens, Georgia: University of Georgia Press, 2000: 231–252.

Tate, Mary Jo. *Critical Companion to F. Scott Fitzgerald: A Literary Reference to His Life and Work*. Facts on File Library of American Literature. New York: Infobase Publishing, 2007.

Turnbull, Andrew, ed. *The Letters of F. Scott Fitzgerald*. New York: Scribner's, 1963.

West, James L.W. III. *The Cambridge Edition of the Works of F. Scott Fitzgerald: Last Kiss*. Cambridge University Press, 2017.

www.ingramcontent.com/pod-product-compliance
Lightning Source LLC
LaVergne TN
LVHW011051110826
845149LV00015B/3461

* 9 7 9 8 9 9 4 5 2 2 6 0 8 *